WHERE'S WALRUS?
AND PENGUIN?

BY STEPHEN SAVAGE • SCHOLASTIC PRESS • NEW YORK

FOR MY DAUGHTER, CHLOË

With special thanks to my wife, Stefanie Wood;
my agent, Brenda Bowen; my editor, David Saylor;
and everyone at Scholastic

Library of Congress Cataloging-in-Publication Data available
ISBN 978-0-545-40295-8

10 9 8 7 6 5 4 3 2 1   15 16 17 18 19
Printed in Malaysia 108   First edition, September 2015

The artwork was drawn and created digitally.
The title type was hand-lettered by Stephen Savage.
The display type and text type were set in
Eunoia Regular and Gotham Book.
Book design by Stephen Savage and David Saylor